To Pat –
Who gave me my
1st Book on
Siamese –
Much love,
Tammy

CATSONG

T.J. Banks

D0998871

PublishingWorks
Exeter • New Hampshire • 2006

Published by:

PublishingWorks
60 Winter Street
Exeter, NH 03833
603-778-9883
www.publishingworks.com

Ordering:
Revolution Booksellers
60 Winter Street
Exeter, NH 03833
800-738-6603
www.revolutionbooksellers.com

Some of the essays have been previously published in *Guideposts' Soul Menders, Their Mysterious Ways, Touched from Above*, and *So Many Miracles* as well as in *laJoie, Just Cats!* and on the website www.cleverkitty.org.

LCCN: 2006903041
ISBN: 1-933002-22-0
ISBN-13: 978-1-933002-22-4

For all the cats who have graced our lives but especially for the original Gang of Seven — Cricket, Kilah, Dervish, Tikvah, Zorro, Woody, and Boris — and, of course, for my Summer Solstice, who was as magical as her name.

Acknowledgments

As a writer, I've been blessed with incredibly thoughtful, responsive editors: Nancy and Bob Hungerford of *Just Cats!;* Rita Reynolds of *laJoie;* Phyllis Hobe of Guideposts' *Listening to the Animals* and *Comfort from Beyond* series and *Their Mysterious Ways* (also from Guideposts); and Kim Cady of cleverkitty.org. I have learned so much from all of you, and I value your friendship and support more than I can say. Thanks, too, to Gertie McClinchey for bringing *Catsong* to life through her vivid illustrations. And a special thanks to Jeremy Townsend of PublishingWorks who has believed in this book from the beginning and who has done everything possible and then some to make it happen.

Many thanks, too, to Thomas D. Morganti, DVM, and the entire staff of the Avon Veterinary Clinic, past and present, and to Mary Ellen Hape and the late Kenneth Hape of Singin' Cattery. You are all part of the warp and weft of these stories.

And, saving the best for last, I want to thank my daughter, Marissa Spooner, a writer to be reckoned with, for coming up with the Prologue's dialogue. It's funny, it's inspired, and it has the A. B. Aby Seal of Approval.

CONTENTS

Prologue

Rory—aka Aurora Borealis, aka A. B. Aby—looks up at me from the breezeway radiator, where she's baking herself. Her enormous yellow eyes are even more enormous. *Can I have a story written about me? Can I? Can I? C'mon!*

"Maybe," I tell her. She's hard to resist.

Rory ponders this. *But I broke your ankle.* She looks poutier than ever, which is no easy trick, considering that pouty is her workaday expression.

"That's not helping your case."

I'll break the other one if I don't get a story written about me. She would, too. For a long time now, I've suspected that she somehow got those long spoon-shaped paws of hers on the X-rays of the ankle that I broke trying *not* to trip over her on the cellar steps. She probably brings them out at parties to show the other cats.

"Are you resorting to threatening?" I ask.

Rory nods her Blue Aby head.

I will write about her eventually, of course. She's too much of a personality to ignore, this Siamese-in-an-Abyssinian-suit of ours. But, then, one way or another, they all wander, paw, and meow their way into my writing. It all started with a lanky red tabby named Alexander....

— *T. J. Banks. Dialogue by Marissa Spooner.*

1

GEM. 06

My Czar Cat

He sat on the old kitchen table, a lanky red tabby. Definitely full-grown. Like the table, he had been somebody's discard. He was nothing like the cuddly yellow kitten that my grandmother had promised me.

We looked each other over. Despite his skinniness and blatant lack of pedigree, he had an aristocratic manner. Somehow my almost-nine-year-old mind got the notion that I should greet him as any cat worth his whiskers would want to be greeted: I went over to him and gently rested my cheek against him. He rubbed his face against my hair, showing me that he understood. From then on, he was my kindred spirit in a fur suit.

Of course, I already had a cat—we all had cats, most of them shanghaied from our grandparents' farm—but Sandy was skittish, almost feral around humans. So, a few weeks earlier, my grandmother had promised me one of the kittens who were always lurking behind the hay bales in the barn. My father and I had gone up one Friday afternoon, after he got home from work, to pick up the kitten, only to find out that a cow had stepped on it, killing it instantly.

A week or so later, Dad had been rushed to the hospital with a heart attack. The next morning, Craig, Gary, and I had been left off at the farm while Mom and our older brother, Marc, had headed to the hospital. My grandmother, wanting to comfort me, had come up with the only solution she could think of: a kitten. Flipping through the local weekly paper, she'd hit on an ad for free kittens. "A yellow one or a black one?" she'd asked Craig once she'd gotten hold of the person who'd placed the ad.

"Yellow," he'd quickly replied, and Alexander came into

3

my world.

Alexander helped me get through the next few weeks till Dad came home from the hospital. He took to waiting with me at the bus stop in the morning. I'd pick him up, and he'd let me hold him for awhile; then, being an upwardly mobile kind of cat, Alexander would leap from my arms to the top of my head. He'd sit there, lordly in his stripes, checking out the traffic patterns, and I, little nut job that I was, would be standing by the stone lamppost in the front yard, wearing this full-grown cat like a bizarre stovepipe hat.

When the school bus came back around in the afternoon, he'd be sitting alongside the driveway, waiting. He was the first cat who was all mine, comforting me whenever I was sick or lonely. Mirabel Cecil's book *Lottie's Cats* was light years away in my future—I didn't happen upon it till my daughter, Marissa, was a baby—but, like Lottie, I already knew that some cats were magical. Alexander, in my eyes, had more magic up his paw than most.

I brought him to my school pet show, where he won a blue ribbon for "The Longest Tail." I put—I'm ashamed to admit this now—doll clothes on him, and he let me. I drew pictures of him and wrote stories in which he fought vampires and other beasties and things that went bump in the night. (I was a big Dark Shadows fan). As he grew older and filled out, his tabby coat turned a warm autumnal golden-red, set off by his white cravat and gloves. He looked positively regal—ergo, his new name, Czar Alexander Meshuganov.

Alexander was very playful. Whenever Craig practiced his golf shots in the front yard, Alexander was there. As soon as the putter hit the ball, he'd be on it—literally—and Craig would be out another golf ball. Alexander also took it upon himself to help Craig with his insect collection for science class, crunching down on grasshoppers with true gourmet gusto.

He had a sense of humor, too. Once, he followed my brother Gary out to the field. Gary, who happened to have some string on him, began dragging it through the grass. Alexander, of course, pounced on it. Gary began running downhill with the string (the field was anything but flat), only to realize after a few moments that the paw-tugging on the other end had stopped. He whipped around and saw Alexander sitting at the top of the slope, just watching. *That was fun. Let's try it again, kid— with feeling this time.*

My Czar-Cat was also a lady's man. He took off regularly to squire the various she-cats in the neighborhood, and a goodly percentage of the kitten crop at our house alone (this was before the majority of folks realized the importance of spaying and neutering) sported red tabby markings in varying degrees. One long-haired tortoiseshell kitten, Sassy, had half-a-red tabby face.

Once Alexander had had his pick of the females-in-residence—the ladies found his stripes and his low-pitched melancholy miaow irresistible—he'd vanish. Then, just as suddenly, he'd be back, climbing the screen door and crying to be let in. Or I'd wake up during the night to find him serenading me from the wall under my window.

When he disappeared in the early spring of my last year of junior high, I figured that he was off on another one of his rendezvous. As the days turned into weeks, however, I began to worry. I searched the fields, then sadly faced facts. My beloved Czar-Cat was gone, taking with him all the magic he'd brought into my child's world.

Years later—I was in college by this time—my mother and I pulled into a parking lot and saw a red tabby moseying about. "Looks like Ali," I said, falling back on one of my nicknames for my old friend. I added jokingly, "Maybe it is Ali."

Mom threw me an odd look. "You don't still believe—"

"No," I replied. "He just *looks* a lot like Ali."

Then Mom blurted out the whole story. Craig had gone out one morning and found Alexander lying dead behind the toolshed. "We can't tell her," Dad had said when he'd heard the news. "It would break her little heart." So Alexander had been buried quietly behind the shed. "It was for the best," Mom assured me hastily.

"No, it wasn't," I retorted angrily, remembering the heartsick child combing the field. "I spent three weeks looking for him!"

Still, the truth had, as they say, set me free. The painfulness of that long-ago but very real loss was gone now that I knew Alexander hadn't left me willingly. Death had, in all probability, come for him quickly. *He had* seemed oddly listless for a week or so before his "disappearance," and we had never known how old he truly was.

Chemistry—kindred spirits, soul mates, call it what you will—is a funny thing. There's no dictating it. Somehow two souls knit together and stay knitted together, no matter what. Even death cannot undo those ethereal skeins. Every time I see a red tabby, I remember the cat who gave himself wholeheartedly to a child, and who taught her the importance of speaking Cat. Those are things that have shaped me, that I bring with me each time I let a new cat into my life.

Seems that Alexander left some of his magic behind, after all.

Jason

The long-haired black-and-white stray was moseying around our backyard again. I watched him from the kitchen window for a few moments. "Looks like Jason," I murmured to my husband and an old high school friend who was visiting us.

Karen came over to the window. "It does," she agreed.

Tim joined us. Despite his jokes about Jason's weight ("So, when are you going to cook that cat? Could feed a family of eight."), my husband had been very fond of him. "Just like a Stephen King novel," he remarked. He made his voice go spooky. "The same but not the same . . ."

Jason came to me the same day that my beloved Sealpoint Siamese, Christy, died. "You have to get another cat right away," my friend Priscilla urged me, "or you won't ever." We found Jason via the local newspaper flyer—in fact,   it was the same publication in which my grandmother had found the ad for Alexander, and the same one that would lead me to Derv many years later. By early evening, a kitten, all long hair and tuxedo markings, was toddling over to where I was lying on my parents' living-room carpet. He hopped up on me and stretched out full-length along my throat. I was His Now, he informed

7

me solemnly, and went to sleep. It had, after all, been a long, tiring day for him.

Jason didn't give me a lot of time for grieving. He didn't fill Christy's place so much as he created one of his own. Wherever I was, there he was, a tubby little black-and-white kitten with a feathery tail and a single agenda. One day, he got bored with the stairs and decided to go for the quicker over-the-railing route. Unfortunately, he misjudged the distance and landed tail-end-up in the wastebasket at the foot of the stairs. When I rescued him, he just stared at me, his yellow eyes beseeching. *"You won't tell anyone about this, will you? Any other cats, I mean?"*

He slept down in the cellar. I'd sit down there with him for a while some nights, and his nightly ritual was, as far as I could tell, pretty much the same: he'd carefully choose a sock from the dirty laundry basket (for some reason, he preferred men's socks), then carry it in his mouth over to the clean laundry basket, hop in, and go to sleep. Apparently, the sock served as his teddy bear or security blanket. In the mornings, as soon as Dad let him up from the cellar, he'd be at my bedroom door, minus the sock and miaowing.

Jason grew into an imposing eighteen-pound cat with a tail like the ostrich plumes sported by fashionable Edwardian women on their hats. Unfortunately, he also picked up some issues along the way, and they weren't as funny or endearing as his nightly sock. He was the first indoor cat we'd ever had (because of her disability, Dad had allowed Christy to live on the large enclosed porch with access to the house, but she'd never had full housecat privileges), and when he was a year and a half old, my parents insisted on having him declawed. To be fair, they honestly didn't know that declawing meant removing part or all of the last bone of each toe; none of us did.

Traumatized, Jason resorted to biting, which made his visits to the veterinary clinic horror movies complete with banshee shrieks, muzzles (which he worked off), and, once, even a restraint pole—until an older, more laid-back vet finally took charge. He simply opened the cardboard carrier, flipped Jason out, did what he had to do, and flipped him back into the carrier. There wasn't even time for a good miaow. Jason had met his match.

Despite all this, Jason could be very lovable and loving. He would curl up on my stomach whenever I had cramps and turn himself into a magnificent tuxedo-style heating pad. He was less than thrilled about my going away to college. I'd start packing, and he'd jump into my suitcase. *"No more room,"* the yellow eyes would inform me. *"Suitcase very full. Guess you'll have to stay."* I'd lift him out and put some sweaters in; he'd hop back in, and I'd pull him back out again. The whole routine would last a good half hour before Jason lumbered off to work on a good sulk.

The suitcase game ended when I decided to take a year off and look for a school closer to home. In the interim, I took some women's studies courses at a local college. Every afternoon, when I got back from classes, Jason would be waiting by the cellar door, miaowing non-stop about his day. He'd sit on my lap while I studied, and took umbrage (he was a very Victorian sort of cat) whenever I had to get up. I was Still His, he informed me, and I Had Better Remember That.

"Look at how he follows Tammy with his eyes," Dad would chuckle as Jason watched me head upstairs to my room.

Dad had more time to notice things like that because he had just retired. Retirement wasn't setting well with him; he wasn't used to not working, and the time just hung on his hands. So, he was delighted when Jason adopted him, too.

Dad had always liked animals, but I never saw him dote on one as he did on Jason. They developed their own little routines, which stayed in place even after Dad went back to work part-time. When Dad went upstairs to change out of his work clothes, Jason trotted behind him, a big furry valet, and he'd trot right back down with Dad, holding his plumy tail high. "C'mon, buddy," my father would say, patting the sofa as he lay down for his afternoon nap. Jason would hop up next to him, not leaving his side for hours. Sometimes they'd even have playful little sparring matches, which made Dad, a former boxer, grin.

If Mom ever had the effrontery to sit down there, the cat would glare at her until she finally felt so uncomfortable that she got up. Jason would then gaze at Dad smugly through half-closed eyes. *Just us guys, right?*

Jason divided his time and affections pretty much between Dad and me. After a while, he mellowed enough to accept a few other humans: Tim, my boyfriend and a born cat lover; and my brother Craig, who was living at home, too. Jason was a "quality-not-quantity" kind of cat, and he liked his inner circle small and select.

That circle got smaller one March night, when Dad suffered a cerebral hemorrhage. He was rushed to the hospital and died there five days later. Jason prowled the house, a lost soul. He'd just sit by the coffee table and stare at the place on the sofa where he and Dad spent many an afternoon, his eyes huge, wistful, and searching . . . or was he seeing something or someone I couldn't? I never was sure which it was, only that there was an uncanny quality to his gaze. Gradually, however, Jason resumed his daily round. I don't think he ever forgot Dad: rather, he, like the rest of us, simply learned to live with the loss.

A few years later, Jason suddenly developed a problem with fluid on his heart. Twice, I brought him to the clinic, sure in my own heart he wouldn't make it. But Jason, like his old buddy, was a fighter—one time, he even bit through the vet's radiation glove—and pulled through both times, spending his convalescence hogging my bed (I'd wake up half-off it, and Mr. Eighteen-Pounder would be lying there with his head on the pillow) and doing a little batting practice (a retired athlete had to keep in shape, after all) with my makeup.

That June, Tim and I got married. Jason stayed with my mother and Craig; he was too old, everyone said, to uproot. Cricket and Kilah, two wild barn kittens, came into our lives shortly afterward. I tried to stop by to see Jason whenever possible. He was always very forgiving. He'd snuggle up against me, tuck his head in the crook of my arm, and nuzzle that arm like the oversized kitten he was.

Early the following November, I got a phone call that Jason was seriously ill. Mom and I rushed him to the clinic. He miaowed weakly once or twice on the way over, but that was it.

The vet on duty found the tell-tale signs of kidney failure. Then she pushed back some of the black fur on his ears: the skin had gone completely yellow. Liver damage, too. At the very least, she said, he would require dialysis, and she didn't recommend it.

Jason managed to scare up a faint hiss. He'd keep on fighting, all right, but he was pitifully weak. I swallowed hard and told the vet that I guessed she'd better put him down.

I was planning to stay with him, of course, and told her so, tearily but emphatically. However, the vet just as emphatically didn't want me present. Sometimes, she explained, the animals sighed, made little noises that upset their owners, etc., etc.

I hugged my old friend gently. As I reluctantly handed him over to the vet, Jason feebly raised one of his white-gloved front paws in an attempt to cuff her. *He* wasn't going gentle into this good night or any other. It was a good way to go out, just as Jason had almost eleven years earlier. His old boxing buddy would've understood.

We brought Jason back to my mother's, and Craig buried him in the side yard, not far from Dad's overgrown garden and Christy's grave. That night, when I came home crampy and depressed, Cricket came to me. She looked at me lovingly with wide kitten eyes and hopped up on my lap. I was Hers Now, she informed me solemnly, and went to sleep. She was stepping into the void, just as Jason had almost eleven years earlier.

Tim and Karen were heading back into the living room now. I took one last look out the kitchen window at the handsome black-and-white stray with the feathery tail and (possibly) a single agenda. I smiled wistfully, turning slowly away. The same but not the same.

Marissa & The "Dats"

My first cat was Smokey, a gray-striped kitten that I cornered in the silage shed on my grandparents' farm. I was seven and delighted: it was the first time I'd ever managed to get my hands on one of those half-wild barn cats. My brother Gary, bent on teasing me, pretended he was going to take the kitten away. I cried, screamed—and held on. Looking back, I'd say it was perfect training for being a freelance writer.

Actually, I only had Smokey for a short time. She never really got over her wildness and ran off when she was about a year old. But she was a part of my life long enough for me to get hooked on cats, and they've been showing up steadily in my life ever since. Our parents never said "No" to any animal we brought home, so Gary and I just kept dragging those cats back with us—zipped up in our jackets, in shoeboxes, and, once, in a cardboard carton on an airplane coming back from Oklahoma. Some cats had a stronger hold on me than others, of course; they are still so real to me all these years later, it seems strange that I cannot turn around and touch them. One of them, a red tabby by the name of Alexander, even waited with me at the bus stop in the morning. In the afternoon, when I got off the bus, he'd be sitting there patiently in all his reddish-gold-striped elegance. We'd share tuna-fish sandwiches together, and he figured in most of my early stories. He and all the others taught me compassion—the need to see things through other than human eyes—and gave me their love and companionship when I was sick and lonely.

Our daughter Marissa is learning the language of cats at an even earlier age than I did. When she cried that first night after my husband Tim and I brought her home from the hospital, the three female cats, Cricket, Kilah, and Tikvah, all hovered around her changing table, making anxious maternal cries. Afterward, they sat in the kitchen and miaowed back and forth about it. Here, they were convinced, was a large odd-looking kitten in distress, and what were the humans doing about it? The males, Dervish and Zorro, behaved in a more traditionally "male" fashion: they got the hell out. Within a week or so, however, "Papa" Derv had rethought his position and taken to sleeping on the rocking chair in Marissa's room. (Either he felt protective of her—he has always had a paternal streak almost as wide as he is—or he'd decided that a rocker with a cozy cushion was too good to waste.) As time went on, he'd go so far as to let Marissa roll all over him and practically use him as a step stool. Sometimes he'd even try to squeeze his nineteen-and-a-half pounds on my lap while I was nursing her.

The other cats began to slowly and cautiously follow suit. Some of the more high-strung ones, Cricket and Tikvah, for instance, wanted a little extra reassurance; but, for the most part, they showed no jealousy of this stranger in their midst. Cricket, who has mothered everything from Derv and Zorro in their kittenhood to her toy soccer balls, began to take an interest in Marissa. She'd let Marissa pat her, even play crazy-kitten games with her catnip toys outside the playpen to amuse her wide-eyed human charge. She would also appear out of nowhere when it was Marissa's bath time and supervise the whole process. Tikvah's interest was less maternal. She liked to sleep on the afghans that were piled up on the bottom

14

shelf of the changing table, and both she and Zorro constantly made off with Marissa's smaller toys. Tikvah would, however, come to get me whenever she heard the baby cry.

Then Woody and Boris joined the household. Woody, alias "the cow cat" (he really does look like a Holstein) wasn't quite full-grown and tried to get in on the bath act. He loves water and often can be found licking raindrops off the cat enclosure's chicken-wire fencing. Cricket, however, took her duties as governess-cat very seriously and always chased him off. Boris, a battle-scarred red tabby whom we originally called "Mr. Will-Purr-for-Food," took one look at Marissa and decided that she was his ticket into the house. Almost immediately, he attached himself to her. He'd let her lie on him, squeeze him teddy-bear style, and even pull out bits of his fur. If he felt she was really getting out of line, he'd turn around and give me or Tim a nip. It was almost, Tim said, as if he was saying to us, "Mind your kitten."

Marissa is almost two years old now. She adores her "dats" or "keddies" and runs after them eagerly, chuckling delightedly whenever she manages to touch one. The cats, for their part, would prefer to love her from a judicious distance. Cricket has given up supervising the after-lunch baths—Marissa splashes too much now—but she and the others still watch her with curiosity. And, even though her increased mobility has literally made them jumpy, they all have their preferred sleeping spots in her room.

Not long ago, I happened to peer into Marissa's room while she was napping and saw Boris sleeping right next to the crib. Boris bears little resemblance to Alexander: he's stockier than the old czar-cat and lacks the latter's gentleman-cat-about-town elegance. But his fur is the same shade of reddish-gold, and the sight of him there brought back memories of that other tabby who was always there for another, older child. I stood in the doorway for awhile, satisfied in knowing that Marissa had, if not a czar-cat, at least a buddy who would come to mean as much to her as my old friend had meant to me.

Shadow & Soul

I am sitting at my word processor, staring tiredly at the lines on the screen. Words that were flame-vivid to me just a short time before now feel lifeless. I've lost the magic, that sense of being spellbound by my fictional dream. I push my chair back and wonder why I sit alone in this room day after day, trying to weave all these words and images together. Then I hear a meow-ow and feel a paw on my shoulder. I turn my head slightly, and there is Cricket, balancing on her back paws ballerina-style on the edge of the desk behind me. She stares at me, her amber eyes large and anxious. Then she jumps down from the desk, scurries over to my worktable, and makes a bold leap for kittykind onto the top of the monitor. She dangles her velvety white paws over the screen and gazes at me, purring. I am no longer alone. I scritch her ears, play with her front paws a bit, and start typing again.

Cats and writing go together for me; both have been a part of my life for as long as I can remember. Writing is a lonely, demanding business, and cats are especially good at supplying the quiet companionship—and comic relief—that we writers need so badly. All seven of our cats are curious about the word processor, but Cricket, chief editor-cat, regards it as her particular property. Back when she was a runty, big-eared gray-ish-brown tiger kitten, she used to make a point of sitting on my lap while I was typing, her eyes lighting up as she pressed one key after another, and sometimes all of them at once. My husband Tim and I would make jokes about the book she was trying to write. I had more typos than usual in my stories and articles, but Cricket seemed satisfied with the results.

Nowadays she's mostly content to stretch out on the floor or on the printer while I work, waiting for me to take a break and drag her long-tailed catnip critters around for her. The best editors, she clearly believes, should know enough to kick back during the creative process.

I think of her as my soul because sometimes she reads me better than I do. Cricket senses when I'm lonely or just plain having a case of writer's blues. She stays with me then, rubbing her face against mine and making little concerned noises. She'll curl up in my lap or on the table next to me, one white-gloved paw curled around my finger, and purr until my dark mood passes. At night, she snuggles up close to me, *squunking* happily. (A *squunk* is somewhere between a purr and a sigh, and it's the most contented, soothing noise, especially on those nights when my chronic insomnia is winning the war.)

Cricket and Tikvah (which is Hebrew for "hope") are inseparable in my mind—partly because they look so much alike and partly because they both need so much more love and reassurance than the other cats. Cricket, the runt of the litter, had, and still has, a strong need to be stroked and held. Tikvah, a former stray, still carries the emotional scars of that life, and is easily startled or frightened. Tim calls her "a big complex with claws," and there's more than a little truth to the description.

Tikvah was living out in my mom's field with a single look-alike kitten when I first saw her. Something about the sight of this mom fending for her kitten and herself grabbed at my cat-susceptible heart, and I immediately started putting out food for them. The kitten either died or took off on its own after a few months, but Tikvah kept coming around, torn between her desire for food and affection and her fear of people. After a few months, she'd let me stroke her head; if I tried to pick her up, however, she'd struggle, her double-paws flailing every which way. I learned to wait and let her come to me.

One day, about seven months after she started showing up for meals, Tim and I caught her and brought her home with us. She was sick. Very sick. Her light-gray fur with the darker gray stripes and soft orange shadings—kitty highlights, I suppose you could call those touches of orange scattered throughout her thick coat—was dull and lifeless; so were her large green owl eyes. She had worms, cystitis, and bronchitis so severe, it sounded like she was about to rip apart at the seams every time she coughed. She was not, Tim insisted, going to live with us; we already had three cats at the time, and I couldn't keep giving in to what he called my "Mother Teresa complex" whenever a homeless feline came my way. I made a few efforts to place her, but my heart wasn't in it. I couldn't think about letting Tikvah go to anyone, friend or stranger, without feeling horribly guilty. In her own funny, hesitant way, she'd begun to trust me, and giving her away would have broken that trust. Then, too, Tikvah was such a nervous, defensive cat that I was afraid very few people would put up for long with the way she had of suddenly, unexpectedly striking out with those extra claws of hers.

Of course, she ended up staying with us. She already had me smack in the middle of her very capable double-paws, and Tim, despite all his talk, was as much of a mush about the cats as I was. So she lucked out, as our vet, Tom, told her. Or, as Rod, an old bus-driver friend of mine put it when I told him Tikvah's story and what her name meant, "Because she *had* hope." I started to say no, that wasn't quite it—we'd named her "Tikvah" because she'd *needed* hope—but then stopped myself. I suddenly saw that Rod was right—"Tikvah" had been the right name for her because she'd had hope come to her in the form of two offbeat cat-crazed humans who didn't know how to walk away and leave "well enough" alone.

For her, it was like having a second chance at kittenhood. She had food and stand-up radiators and even a waterbed to snooze on (although still, when she hears a thunderstorm or even a good, fierce wuthering wind, she'll wake up out of a sound sleep, her green eyes wide with fear and remembering). She had toys, which she hoarded happily under the coffee table. She even had other cats to hang out with, once she felt less threatened by them. Tikvah wasn't too sure about us, though. She liked being petted, yes; but she'd also learned at some point in her previous life that human hands could hurt you, and she was wary.

Two years and a lot of love and patience later, Tikvah has finally begun to trust us. [the tenses in this are confusing. Maybe make it all past tense?] Sometimes she still claws and nips when she really means to nuzzle or play, and she still gets frightened if Tim or I try to pick her up. She shadows me around the house a good part of the day and evening, though, and constantly butts her head against our hands for attention. She has even become a snuggler—on her own terms. If I am lying quietly on the sofa under her favorite afghan, she'll hop up and stretch out full-length alongside or on top of me. If I move, however, even if it's just the tiniest fraction,   she'll   jump down and scurry out of the room.

If Cricket is my soul, then Tikvah is my shadow, and not just because of the way she trails me about. She is my shadow-self, the fearful one in each of us that wants to trust but pulls back, remembering past hurts and bruises. She has taught me that trust—whether it's the trust of a human who finds it hard to let his soul-wounds heal or of a stray cat who has never known gentleness or love before—comes even more slowly and silently than Carl Sandburg's cat-footed fog; that it involves holding one's self still, and listening.

The Best Bet

"Huh, she turned out better'n I expected," my uncle said, studying the almost full-grown dark-gray tiger cat by the open cellar door. "I never thought that gray one would amount to much."

My husband, Tim, and I had snagged Cricket and her sister Kilah from my uncle's dairy barn not quite a year before. Cricket had been the runt of the litter: a skinny boat-eared bundle of stripes who crept out from behind the hay bales to scarf up some meat scraps only after we'd made off with her showier and bolder sister. Despite her shyness, however, she'd come around before Kilah. Perhaps it was because, as Tim said, she had such a deep need to be touched and held.

She became my cat, snuggling next to me while I read or sitting on my lap while I typed. Cricket fell in love with my typewriter, her green eyes turning suddenly and inexplicably amber at the rapid rise and fall of the keys. Eventually, she took to thwapping the keys with her paws as the spirit moved her, adding a few unexpected characters to my stories. And when the creative energy deserted both of us, we'd hang out on the stairs together in companionable silence. I used to joke that Cricket was my first-born; certainly, I lavished as much care and attentiveness on her as any mother does on her child. Kilah got her share, make no mistake about it, but it was Cricket whom I coddled, hand-fed, phoned the vet frantically about, and played twig-catch and other games with. She would go to very few other people, often hiding on top of the cupboards in the cellar when strangers came by and not re-emerging until they'd gone.

We were best buddies. Even when I started using a word processor and she no longer actively contributed to my stories, she'd lounge by my feet, playing with a catnip critter, or drape herself over the monitor, her elegant snow-white paws dangling over the screen. She was a sympathetic listener and, as I've written elsewhere, could read me better than I could read myself, often knowing I was upset before I myself did. She'd follow me all over the house, nuzzling and rubbing up against me anxiously. I'd start wondering what was getting her, and then *click!* I'd realize that it wasn't what was getting her: it was what was getting me, and she, with that feline sixth sense of hers, had picked up on it.

I had a slew of nicknames for her. Secret names. One of them was "Little Bit," a name my vet, Tom, gave her back in her runty days. Even when she grew up big—sometimes too big, as Tom would sternly inform me—and beautiful, the name clung, although it eventually underwent a sea change and became "The Best Bet." She was with me through the best of times and the worst of times. When Tim called me on the day that we were bringing our daughter Marissa home from the hospital, he went so far as to put Cricket on the phone; her rich coffee-perking-in-the-morning purr was a balm and a heart-warmer to a tired new mother recovering from an emergency C-section. And when Tim was killed in a freak car accident a few years later, it was Cricket who quietly and gently brought me back to the land of the living when no human could have possibly reached me.

Early this past spring, Tom noticed that Cricket's "kidney values" were drastically off. We changed her diet, and she seemed to perk up, coming upstairs again to greet me in the mornings (gradually, over the last few months, she'd given up what I now know must have felt like the journey of a thousand steps for her). So I began to push my fear away from me; to believe again that my best beloved, my kindred sprit in stripes, would be communing on the stairs with me for years to come.

Then, on the second anniversary of Tim's death, I took her to the vet for her monthly weigh-in. She was still a big girl, but she'd lost a noticeable amount of weight.

"She looks fine," my friend Cel tried to reassure me when she came by in the evening. She stroked the brownish-gray fur with its reddish undertone—it had gradually deepened and changed its hue over the eleven years she had been with me—that Cricket was so vain of. She'd always gloried so much in being brushed that Tim and I used to joke that she should have a standing appointment at the hairdresser's. "Her coat feels good." Cel smiled. "She looks like she should be sitting on top of a mountain and little kittens should be climbing up to ask her the meaning of life."

By the next morning, though, Cricket had gone from being the Buddha-Cat to simply being a very sick critter. She threw up on one of her front paws and couldn't summon up the strength to clean it off until later in the day. Even then, she couldn't launder it to its usual snowy whiteness. She kept to the downstairs bathroom and didn't even hiss or growl when Starfire, the Siamese upstart whom she loathed, tried to invade the premises. She wouldn't eat or drink. I gave her water through an eye dropper, smeared malt-flavored hairball remedy on her gums, made an appointment with Tom for Monday, when the clinic would open again, and prayed.

It didn't take Tom long to size up the situation. "I think she's getting ready to close up shop," he said gently, adding that, given what he'd seen in the spring, he hadn't really expected her to hold out this long. He looked at Marissa and me. "I'll give you some time alone."

I tried to explain to five-year-old Marissa what was going to happen so that she wouldn't be frightened. Then I laid my cheek against that beautiful velveteen coat for the last time and whispered all her secret names to her, letting her go. And I kept my hands on her as Tom gave her that last shot and she made her way out of this world, leaving behind a beloved but empty shell.

I have two books about animals as teachers and healers lying beside me right now—books I'm looking forward to reading and learning from. But Cricket taught me more than any book ever could. I learned that a cat can give you more love and understanding than I once could ever have dreamed of. And that, given that same love and understanding in return, a people-shy gray-striped runt with sailboat ears that nobody thinks will amount to much can become The Best Bet.

Tikvah

When I first knew Tikvah—way back in the days when she was a stray who roamed the field behind my mom's house and kept a pantry full of mice in the old toolshed—I used to see her sitting like that in the yard, looking, for all the world, like she was checking for rain, which she probably was.

Tikvah was a pragmatist, a down-on-her-luck polydactyl who clearly had known a world of suffering. Not that she could tell us about it, of course. But after she came to live with Tim and me, we'd notice little (or not-so-little) telltale signs, such as her absolute I'm-digging-my-claws-into-you-sucker-and-taking-you-with-me terror at being picked up. (A lot of my sundresses had some really nice hand-embroidered flowers over the bodices to camouflage the damage she did; "Designs by Tikvah," we used to call the results.) Or the way she'd bolt from her favorite radiator perch whenever she saw me pull the broom out of the closet. Tim and I didn't want to know or even think about what had been done to her with a broom, but he muttered a few comments about what should be done to the so-called human or humans who'd abused her, and I tried not to bring the broom out when she was around. She was, in short, as Tim used to say, "a big complex with claws."

She was also an extremely opinionated cat who made a point of airing her "opinionations" (my word) whenever possible, which led to another Tim-ism: "Tik-Talk." "OK, now it's time for "Tik-Talk,'" he'd announce, using a special voice he'd created just for her. It was kind of a George-Bush-Meets-the-Wicked-Witch-of-the-West voice. That sounds bizarre, but it utterly suited her. In fact, if Tikvah *could've* spoken to us in human-ese, I wouldn't have been at all surprised if she'd come out with that very voice.

As far as the other cats were concerned, Tikvah was strong medicine. *Very* strong medicine. Her distrust extended to her own species as well. In all her years with us, she only loved one of her fellow felines; that was Cricket, who resembled her enough physically and in personality that Tikvah clearly regarded her as a soul sister. She viewed everybody else in a fur suit with her usual double-pawed ambivalence, and that meant she had to hit them. You know—get them before they got her. *It's just on general principle,*[what's that mean?] *you understand, she seemed to be saying. The other cats understood only too well.*

Of course, in the beginning, we had to scold her for her unprovoked attacks on her species. Tikvah would look at us gravely out of those pale-green owl eyes of hers—you could almost see her nodding—and bide her time. The moment that Dervish or Kilah was getting reamed out for clawing the furniture, Officer Tikvah would materialize out of nowhere and begin whacking the kitty crap out of them.

There were a couple of variations on this particular theme, and one of them had to do with the fact that Tikvah did not like being caught being nice. Sometimes during that first year, for instance, I'd look up from the book I was reading and see her surreptitiously washing the top of Kilah's head while the latter was sleeping. The instant Tikvah felt my eye upon her, she'd get all flustered and start smacking the other cat alongside the head. Poor Kilah would wake up looking very dazed, very confused, while her assailant glared at me. *That didn't mean anything,* Tikvah would assure me and hop off the bed.

What didn't mean anything? Kilah would want to know, still shaking her aching head and looking like a hit-and-run victim—which was, when you got right down to it, essentially what she'd *been*.

"Never mind," I'd say, patting her. "Go back to sleep."

The second variation only occurred once that I know of, and it involved Dervish and Tikvah's ovaries. Or, rather, a particle of one of her ovaries. She'd been in heat when she'd been spayed; because of the swelling (we'd actually thought she was pregnant at the time), a piece of an ovary about the size of my little fingernail had gotten left in the works, sending her back into heat off and on. Tikvah had to be—I kid you not—re-spayed. In order not to do a déjà vu number here, however, we had to wait until the "heat," and Tikvah, were at their worst point. This meant a lot of rolling and writhing on our usually no-nonsense girl's part. At one point, she actually propositioned Derv on the kitchen table, not realizing (or not caring) that he had been neutered at an extremely early age. Derv watched her maneuvers with raised eyebrows (well, really they were tiny, slightly curved orange stripes over his eyes—part and parcel of his tabby markings—but, as my brother Marc said, they *looked* like eyebrows). Finally, in anger and despair, Tikvah rose to her paws and swatted the poor guy full in the face. *What good are you?* her eyes scathingly demanded before she did a haughty exit, stage right, from the table.

Ergo, my nicknames for her—"The Iron Paw" and "Butt-a-bingster." The latter had its origins with Pam, a half-Italian, half-Jewish girl I'd known back at Lehigh University who'd used her hands so fully, so *vividly* in conversation, it had been a trip just to *watch* her talk. "So I slapped him—*butt-a-bing!*" she'd relate, hands flying back and forth as they underscored the action in her story. Somehow I had a feeling that Tikvah would have found Pam a soul sister,.

Tim—who, along with his gift for mimicry, bad jokes, and worse puns, also had a gift for making up bizarre or offbeat lyrics to songs just like that—*snap!*—had to take it a step further, of course. He gave Tikvah and her significant paws their very own theme song:

"I am Tikvah, hear me roar,
With paws too big to ignore . . ."

If Cricket was the only cat Tikvah ever allowed herself to feel close to, then I was her sole human compadre. We understood each other. I didn't find loving and trusting easy things to do either; just as my Butt-a-bingster would stand up prairie-dog-style, trying to determine whether she could make the jump onto that tall bureau or that really high shelf, I had to sit back and gauge situations before making my leaps of faith.

Because I understood her, I never swooped down on her to scoop her up into my arms (unless, of course, she was due at the vet's for shots) or forced her into lap-cat habits. "She really doesn't like being picked up," I'd caution cat-loving friends who were intent on making friends with my big-pawed girl. Usually, they'd ignore me and end up finding out the hard scratchy way the truth of what I was saying the hard, scratchy way. I learned that you had to let Tikvah come to you, on her terms, not yours. Since I understood that—and she understood in her own way that I understood that—she would follow me around and burble for me like she would for nobody else.

We lost Tim and Cricket within two years of each other. With Cricket's death, there was an important shift in my relationship with Tikvah. While Kilah, Cricket's sister, became the gang's constitutional monarch, Tikvah took her friend's place as my right-paw girl, my No. 1 familiar. She had a different way of showing her love than Cricket had had, but, as I learned in the three years that followed, it held just as strong and true, even when, in that last year, arthritis slowed her down drastically.

29

Slowed her down, yes, but didn't stop her completely. Not, as old Iron-Paws herself would've been the first to say, on your—and, trust me, could she have spoken, her emphasis would most certainly have been on "your"—life. A month or so after arthritis had begun to curtail her policing activities, (she spent more and more time on an orthopedic kitty bed on her favorite shelf in the cellar, eating specially prepared meals on one of those acrylic-covered kitchen savers) she would still hobble upstairs periodically to inspect the troops and rip out (no slow painstaking weeding for Tikvah) any insurrection in the ranks. On one such expedition, Starfire, the young Siamese prima donna, came waltzing over to Tikvah with a big kitty smirk on her elegant Sealpoint face. Clearly—Star is not a subtle feline, never has been, never will be—she was itching to show the old lady who was boss now.

The old lady gave Star a long, hard "you-haven't-even-begun-to-earn-your-stripes-yet-Private" look. Star blanched—or would've if she could have—and backed off immediately. *Er—excuse me—I seem to remember I have some bugs I have to chase,* her expression said as she booked.

Tikvah sat there for some time after the Siamese had fled. She looked very pleased with herself. *Showed that foreigner, didn't I? Still got it.*

Did she ever. The story must've gone the rounds, because none of the younger cats ever tried to mess with General Tikvah again. The insurrection stemmed, Tikvah seemed to enjoy her semiretirement on the "apartment" shelf she sometimes shared with Kilah and Dervish. She was never as close to them as she had been to Cricket, but they were old cronies now and had seen cats and kittens come and go. I could just imagine them reminiscing *(Say, do you remember when that mole got into the house, and we all went charging after it . . . ?)* and playing kitty bingo, as my vet, Tom, said.

Sometimes Tikvah would still head up to the second floor to soak up the sun in Marissa's room, but, more often than not, I'd go down to the cellar and, stepping onto a chair (the shelf was a high one), reach up and pat her. She was still, I assured her, my special girl. And while my fingers would be smoothing that pussy willow--colored fur of hers with its soft orange-y tinge, the same image kept coming into my mind: that of a limber, vibrant Tikvah making her way across a sunlit field.

Maybe—just maybe, I thought—it's a memory from the days before she came to live with us. But a long time afterward, my friend Rita said, "Maybe she was trying to prepare you."

Maybe she was. A few months later, she went off her food all of a sudden. If she doesn't start eating by tomorrow, I told myself on the second night, I'll take her in to see Tom.

When the next morning came, I found her lying on her side on the cellar floor, still breathing but obviously in great pain. She looked up at me, and her eyes said it all: *I can't do this any more.*

I dropped off my daughter Marissa at a friend's house and headed over to the clinic with Tikvah in the carrier on the seat beside me. Once there, I didn't hurry to take her in, just sat there, singing softly along to one of my favorite Bill Staines songs and talking to her. When the song was done, I simply pressed the rewind button and played it again, touching her face gently through the carrier's grid door. For that moment, we were outside of time, and I wanted to keep it that way as long as possible.

Because once we were inside the examination room, time began moving all too quickly. "Renal lymphoma," Tom said, feeling her abdomen carefully. "There was no sign of it when she was in four months ago, but, then, it moves quickly in older cats."

There was no question in either of our minds as to what

had to be done. The pain that had her in its grip would be even more excruciating in a day or so. She'd had a long life with us, longer than she would've had if she had not chosen to push past her fear of humans and let herself find haven with us for eleven years.

"You want to stay?" Tom asked me. It was really a rhetorical question.

I nodded. Except in Jason's case, I had always stayed with my animals till the end, believing that I owed them that much. In Tikvah's case, it mattered all the more to me. I did not want her to go out of this world feeling alone and abandoned, as she'd been when I'd found her in my mother's field.

Still, when the moment came and Tom's hand was gently, quietly bringing down the needle for that last shot, I, who had been through this with so many other cats and dogs without crying, no matter how deeply the grief had cut, cried. Not great big gulping sobs, mind you, just little tears that spattered against my cheeks like raindrops against a windowpane. Even for Cricket, my "best beloved" cat, I hadn't cried like that because tears, like love, just don't come easily to me. But for my old general-cat, my Tikvah-bus, I cried.

You taught me so much, I told her silently, tightening my hold on her. And just as the needle grazed her leg, she turned her head toward me, fastening her round green eyes on me with that peculiar fierce tenderness she'd shown precious few souls in her life. Even after the injection had done its work, those eyes did not close in a peaceful death-sleep, as I'd seen so many other animals' eyes do. No, they remained open and fixed on me. I pressed my hands lovingly against her body and, incred-

32

ibly, felt a deep purr vibrating through it.

I mentioned this to Tom. He shook his head. "No," he told me kindly, "she was gone at once." Sandy, my friend and confidante at Orphan Alley, a no-kill shelter in Gresham, Wisconsin, had another take on the subject, though. "You and Tikvah had such a close bond," she wrote me as soon as she'd received the news, "that it isn't surprising that you felt her communicate with you even after her heart stopped beating. Those bonds are forever."

Don't I know it. Sometimes, when I'm down in the cellar, I'll suddenly swivel around for no reason; no reason except that my heart expects to see a pair of ever-watchful pale-green owl eyes peering down at me from that shadowy shelf hangout of hers.

*****

A few months after Tikvah hung up her double-pawed boxing gloves and went toward the light—I could just see her standing up on her hind legs, trying to determine whether she could go the distance in a single leap—a friend and I were having a half-playful, half-serious discussion about what she was up to in the hereafter. I said I thought she'd been given a post at the gates of Cat Heaven; there, she got to decide which felines got in and which ones had to go back and "try again." She did, of course, get to bop the latter back down to this earthly plane—which, knowing Tikvah as I did, I figured she must enjoy doing.

"It would be a sheer waste of administrative ability otherwise," she agreed.

Whatever she's up to in the Great Kitty Beyond, however, I know exactly what my old girl will do when I catch up with her, say, fifty or sixty years from now. She'll come running to me through a field of long-tall celestial grasses shimmering green-gold in the sunlight. She'll stop just before she reaches me, sit down on her haunches, and look at me thoughtfully; then slowly, she'll raise a front paw in greeting. And this time, in her owl eyes, I will see only joy and love, for the former things—the fear, the abuse, and the near-starvation—will have passed away.

The House Blessing

A lot of times, as I found out, you get a half-Abyssinian which is not a bad thing, mind you. But sometimes you get the whole Abyssinian.

I had wanted an Abyssinian cat ever since I'd read Gladys Taber's *Amber: A Very Personal Cat*. Granted, we did have Zorro, a charcoal-gray Aby-tabby mix ("We can always sell him as a rare black Abyssinian," my husband Tim used to say) who had wandered into our yard when he was eight-weeks old and who, after checking our house out, had decided we were worth staying with. Despite his coloring and the conspicuous tabby stripes on his mottled coat, he had the agility, dexterity, (he's the only one of our cats who has ever figured out that he needed to put his paw *around* a doorknob to make Things Happen), and highly intuitive way of communicating with people that, as I later learned, marked his purebred relations.

But my Abyssinian dream seemed destined to remain just that. After Tim's death, I went to a Cat Writer's Association (CWA) conference out in California and stopped in at the cat show next door. I found myself lingering by the Aby cages; later, I returned to the room I was sharing with my fellow cat writer Sally Bahner and sheepishly took a handful of Aby breeder cards out of my pocket.

"I think it's a sign for you to get an Abyssinian cat," Sally remarked with amusement.

I chose to ignore the sign then, but the Abys found me anyhow. They're very determined that way. Watch them at a show sometime and notice how they keep trying to jimmy those locks on their cages. Three years later, I hooked up with a couple of

35

Aby breeders, one of whom, Mary Ellen Hope, became a good friend and mentor. From her cattery, Singin', came Damiana, a blue Aby kitten whom my cattery, Damiana-z, was named for, and Celtic Fire (a.k.a. Celtie), a Red Abby spay. From another out-of-state cattery came an amber-eyed Ruddy kitten whom my daughter Marissa and I saddled with a name bigger than she was: Summer Solstice.

From the beginning, Solstice was an odd mixture of shyness and playfulness. She came across as being more self-effacing, less people-oriented than either Damiana or Celtie; but she was also the wise guy kitten, the one who always started the wrestling matches and playfights. She was undersized and fighting an upper respiratory infection that just wouldn't quit. She'd go around the house making these snuffling snort-hog noises, which sounded bizarre coming from such a dainty feminine-looking kitten. Despite this, she managed to acquire an ardent beau in Topaz, our young Flamepoint Siamese. He was, and is, nuts about all our Aby girls; their little pointy faces and Dumbo ears apparently make his heart sing. But Solstice with her scrappiness and her whiskers that were too big for her cougar face was the Song of Songs, as far as he was concerned.

We lost beautiful big-eyed Damiana to some unforeseen genetic complications a few months before her first birthday. That left Solstice as the sole hope of our cattery. But she wasn't really putting on weight, and Tom, our veterinarian, had a hunch that those snort-hog noises might be due to a polyp in her throat, similar to one he'd removed from Damiana's. His hunch turned out to be uncannily on target: he removed a sizeable polyp and pronounced Solstice ready to go to an upcoming cat show, and then up to Mary's cattery in Rochester, New York, for stud service.

What followed was probably the longest honeymoon in cattery history. Every week for three months, I called Mary for an update on Solstice's romance with a Fawn male, only to learn that there wasn't any.

Truth be told, Solstice sounded as forlorn as any child who'd been sent to summer camp or boarding school against her will: and my heart really did smite me every time Mary told me how pathetically eagerly my little "Cougar-ette" would greet her whenever she came into the room. And long-nosed Topaz ("He looks like Charles DeGaulle," my vet said) wandered around the house, moping for his beloved.

But another, far more serious problem arose. Despite the surgery she'd gone through the previous March, Solstice was having trouble breathing again. A visit to Mary's vet confirmed that the polyp had come back in full force: in view of that fact, there seemed to be no point in putting her through the added stress of breeding. "Spay her," Mary told me over the phone. "Keep her as a pet and just love her."

No problem there. As I was driving up to the Sturbridge cat show a week later to pick Solstice up, I worried, though, that she wouldn't remember us after her three-month honeymoon-that-wasn't-really-a-honeymoon. But when I unlatched her carrier door, Solstice bolted straight out of it and up into my arms.

I knew you'd come, those eloquent amber eyes of hers said. *I knew you wouldn't forget me...*

"I never saw a cat so glad to go home," Mary said emphatically.

One hurdle jumped, two to go. First, there was the biopsy to make sure that the polyp wasn't malignant. *No*, I thought, remembering Damiana with her enormous far-seeing eyes and even more enormous ears, *not this one too.* But the biopsy was negative, and

Tom went ahead with surgery, spaying her and removing a seven-ounce polyp. The wonder wasn't that she'd been going about making those ungodly noises but that she'd been able to *breathe at all.*

She began vacuuming up food. Dry cat food, people food— it didn't matter. Solstice was an Aby with a mission, as far as eating went. *You never know,* the amber eyes would say as she quizzically sniffed a rice cake. By the time her stitches came out, her weight was up to 5.7 – a whole pound heftier than she'd been prior to this last operation.

I believe in signs. And Solstice's complete recovery, coming so soon after the loss of Damiana and several other family pets, was proof positive that we'd finally made our way out of that sad, dark grieving place. There *were* happy endings. Bad things *could* be turned around. And good things *did* happen to good kitties.

On my living room wall is a small gilt-framed piece of poetry entitled "The House Blessing." I never knew who wrote it, but the author certainly knew how to "turn a phrase."

> *God bless the corners of this house,*
> *And be the lintel blest;*
> *And bless the hearth and bless the board*
> *And bless each place of rest;*
> *And bless each door that opens wide*
> *To strangers as to kin;*
> *And bless each crystal window pane*
> *That lets the starlight in;*
> *And bless the rooftree overhead*
> *And every sturdy wall:*
> *The peace of man, the peace of God,*
> *The peace of love on all.*

One morning, oh, maybe a month or two after the surgery, I happened to turn and see Solstice sitting on top of the radiator right under the poem. Always a pretty little cat, she had just then what I could only call a glow, a positive *aura*, that radiated from her big cougar-eyes straight down to her apricot underbelly.

"Are you 'The House Blessing'?" The words were out of my mouth before I realized it.

The amber eyes deepened appreciatively. *I was wondering when you'd notice,* they said gently.

Sometimes you get the whole Abyssinian. And sometimes, as with my little Soul-Cat, you get a miracle.

Catsong

Kilah looks my way as I come down the stairs in the morning. She hobbles out into the kitchen, ignoring the younger cats, and checks out the various food bowls. She eats more than usual: the appetite stimulant that my vet, Tom, gave her last week must be working. In between bites, she talks to me in that oddly Siamese-sounding voice of hers, something that she hasn't done all that often these last few months.

When I open the dishwasher, she hoists the upper part of her almost seventeen-year-old tortoiseshell body onto the door. It's a ritual she started years ago at the old house; after all, you never know when there's going to be margarine or something equally tasty still sticking to the utensils. After a quick look-see, Kilah eases herself back down onto the linoleum. She heads into the spare room, and I follow her, helping her into the litter box. Her arthritis and the mass on her left hind leg make getting in there on her own a little tricky.

Later in the morning, I go back into the room to get started on some painting. I'm almost finished with the first coat on the window frame when I realize I haven't heard that low *"Mer-row"* of hers for a while. *She must be in the living room, soaking up the sun,* I think, then glance down. There's Kilah sitting next to my stepladder, looking up at me. *Did you think I'd go very far away?* her green eyes ask me gently.

It's a good day for my old lady. Last August, Tom removed a cancerous toe from that left hind foot. She came through surgery with her long striped tail waving high and with renewed energy, exploring the upstairs in the new house for the first time. *So, this is your bedroom. Nice,* the eyes said thoughtfully.

She began trailing me down to the cellar on my laundry runs. *Four litter boxes—* Kilah has always had a very expressive face, due in part to her unusual yellow-and-white 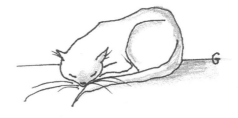 Phantom mask—*and a cat tree. Really. Carpeted down here, too. Much nicer than our old cellar.* Then she'd follow me back upstairs, one slow, careful step at a time, and go nap in the sunny living room with Dervish and Zorro, the other old-timers.

Early this year, I noticed an abrasion on that same paw. Well, sometimes she did scratch herself. Her claws had a tendency to get too long; after all, she didn't move around a lot on account of her arthritis. But the area underneath the abrasion was puffed out and hairless.

Tom wasn't too alarmed at first. But a blood test showed that the cancer was back.

Tom had taken care of our cats ever since my late husband, Tim, and I had brought Kilah and her sister, Cricket, in to him back in their wild little barn-kitten days. That had been more than sixteen years ago. Since then, Tom had seen my daughter, Marissa, and me through personal tragedy and countless animal crises, and it was as both friend and vet that he discussed this new development with me. We were both against putting her through chemo. Nor did he feel that amputation was an option. Kilah was too old to have to suddenly learn to get about on three legs.

"It's a slow-growing malignancy," he told me. "But surgery could cause it to grow faster." Kilah was a strong cat, he assured me; he wasn't ready to write her off yet.

Last Friday, I was carrying Kilah downstairs when my hand felt a mass in her left hind leg. Back to the clinic. The mass had actually been present at her last visit, Tom explained, and it hadn't changed. What worried him was that she'd lost a pound and a half in a month's time, and, as he put it, she didn't have a lot of pounds-and-a-half left to lose. "It's going to happen," he said finally. "Today's not her day, though."

I have never had to help any of my cats "go gentle into that good night" like this. The others were all clearly in severe pain and going downhill rapidly when we made those last trips to the veterinary clinic. Kilah's decline has been slower, less obvious. It's difficult for me to gauge how much she's actually suffering.

Kilah herself is trying so hard, forcing herself to get up, to greet us, to stay with us in body and in spirit as long as possible. *I won't leave you if you still need me,* the beautiful green eyes assure me. Her heart is still strong despite everything. I will have to make the decision for both of us.

Almost seventeen years . . . I can still see the wild little barn kitten who came to us with her equally wild little sister, the two of them wrestling with each other, sleeping on top of each other. Then I see Kilah as she is now, with that incredible love and serenity in her eyes, and a line from Edgar Lee Masters's *Spoon River Anthology* —"*Some beautiful soul that lived life strongly*"—comes to me, and I think how well it suits her. *My old lady is going out in style*, I tell myself.

A week later, however, she's dragging herself from room to room with such obvious discomfort that I can't help wincing for her. Her hindquarters are pitifully gaunt, making her midsection look barrel-like. She rallies later in the day; she eats almost a half-can of her favorite salmon cat food and lies purring by my side on the living-room sofa. Keisha, her adopted daughter, lies on top of me, stretched out in all her blue-tortie glory, touching her nose periodically to Kilah's whiskers in gentle concern. Marissa comes into the room and feels the old cat's body carefully, then leans her head close to her tortoiseshell side. "I think she should go in on Monday," my daughter says in that oddly adult way of hers.

A year ago, when Kilah's health problems started up, I was in a bad place. A lot of things had derailed on me, and I was still picking myself out of the wreckage. I rushed her to the vet early one afternoon, thinking, *Not this, too. Don't die yet—give me one more year.*

There have been so many trips to the clinic together since then. Each time, I've tried to mentally prepare myself for the possibility that this might be the end; each time, she has rallied, and it has been a not-so-minor miracle for me, a sign that things aren't always as bad as they seem.

The day after my talk with Marissa, Kilah rallies one last time. She has what I can only call "The Glow": her coat, which has been so matted and hard to keep up, is suddenly kitten-silky under my fingertips again. She's walking much better, and even the abraded nodule on that hind foot seems to have miraculously healed over. A chill runs through me as I look at her, knowing in my gut that what I'm seeing is a feline version of that inexplicable incandescence that terminally ill people have at the end of their journey. It fades away within the hour, and we continue our deathwatch.

Monday finally comes. Marissa goes to school, and I have my own private good-bye with Kilah before we drive over to the clinic. Stroking her, I realize that it has indeed been just about a year since the day I begged her not to die. "Thank you for keeping your promise and staying that extra year," I tell her simply. "I'll stay with you till the end."

And I do. I wrap my arms around her as she lies on the table and lean in as close to her as I possibly can. Her purr vibrates through her anemic fluid-filled body long after she has left it, leaving me with one last song.

"The end of an era," Tom sighs. He looks down at her. "A beautiful cat—a beautiful spirit."

It's a good epithet.

****

Late one night, maybe two weeks after Kilah's death, I'm having trouble sleeping. I'm just about to settle back down when I hear a low, deep mer-row.

Only one of our cats has ever had a miaow like that. Tim and I used to laugh about it. It was a Lauren Bacall miaow, always sounding like a very insistent *"me now!"*

Of course, what I'm hearing now can't be Kilah.

It comes a second time, then a third. *One of the cats must be stuck somewhere*, I think. Sighing, I swing my legs out of bed, and the rest of me tiredly follows.

I check each room. All of the other cats are fast asleep. There is no logical answer for that *mer-row*.

I've heard it a few times since that night. And I'm aware of a presence—a very gentle, familiar one—that follows me about the house and on my travels. I know, without knowing how I know, that Kilah has not left us yet. I kept my promise about staying with her till the end; she's still keeping hers.

Keisha

She was sitting on top of the cat tree by the pet shop door when we met her, looking for all the world like she'd been waiting for us. *Got my bags packed*, the blue tortoiseshell kitten announced as she hooked me in with her velvety white paw. *What took you so long?*

I, in turn, was entranced. *God, she looks like Dimity!* I thought, reaching out a paw of my own to stroke the orange-flecked blue-gray fur and remembering the shy rag-bag tortoiseshell from my childhood whom I'd chosen over her livelier littermate because . . . because she needed me.

We didn't really need another cat in the here and now—we had nine, which certainly put us past the "gentle sufficiency" point—but the resemblance to my long-lost Dimity was uncanny. There also was that huge hole in our hearts from the death of our beloved Cricket a few weeks earlier. On second thought, maybe we *did* need her, and she, with that even uncannier intuitive ability of hers, knew it before we did.

So it was that Keisha came home with my daughter Marissa and me. Discounted by the pet-store manager—she was ten weeks old, and most folks wanted younger kittens –she fit so easily into our household. The rest of the gang accepted her with barely a hiss (and that hiss came from Star, the Sealpoint Siamese who resented most of her species on general principles). Keisha's personality was uncannily like their late leader Cricket's, and the other cats took to her at once. In fact, she and Bandit, the gorgeous black half-Persian who was a few months her senior, became inseparable, so deeply did he fall in love with her.

But, then, most people were almost as smitten with Keisha as he was. Aside from her wonderful, lush coat–of–many–colors and appealing expression, she had an incredibly sweet personality. She also was a born nurturer, a Florence Nightingale in a fur suit.

When she was about two years old, we had a series of very sweet, very sickly Siamese kittens pass briefly through our lives, bringing a world of love and pain with them. All of them—the two Houdinis and Crystal—had congenital problems; two had to be euthanized, and one, Houdini III, died in his sleep. To watch Keisha with these blue-eyed waifs was a lesson in caring and compassion. She showed a matter-of-fact earth-motherly kindness to each of them, playing with them when they were up for it and just letting them snuggle up against her plushiness when they weren't.

With Houdini II—who was with us for only eleven days before his chronically impacted bowels made it clear that euthanasia was the kindest gift we could give him—she was especially gentle. The other cats, sensing that there was something radically wrong with this kitten, kept their distance. Not Keisha. She let the little guy huddle next to her and soak in as much of her body warmth as he could. He would turn his triangular scrap of a face with its red-gold smudges toward her like she was the Great Cat Sun Goddess and he was an especially grateful flower. *You're so pretty,* his wistful blue eyes said adoringly. *Thank you for being nice to me.*

So strong was this caretaker side of Keisha's personality—so big and beautiful and vibrant was she—that I couldn't imagine her ever being ill or immobilized. She was always the healer, never the one who needed healing. So, when I found her lying horribly still out in the narrow cat-enclosure tunnel one early September day, my mind screamed out in disbelief.

I was sure she was dead, so still was she lying. Numb with

grief, I went inside to get a tool to cut through the chicken wire to remove her body: when I came back, I saw that her sides were moving — not much, but enough that I could let myself breathe again. *It's just the heat,* I quickly reassured myself. *She'll be fine once it cools down.*

But that next morning, Keisha was lying flat-out in the enclosure tunnel again, worse than before. Marissa went into the large walk-in section of the enclosure and, crawling through the narrow cat tunnel, lifted her up onto the platform by the front porch window. We rushed her to the veterinary clinic. Kilah, one of our older cats and Keisha's surrogate mom, seemed a little wobbly on her paws, too, so we brought her along with us.

Tom, our vet, examined both cats carefully. It was, he told us, "some kind of hot *corolla* virus," probably the same one that Bandit had shown signs of having when he'd come in earlier that week. Kilah could go home with us, but there was no question that Keisha would stay. She was running a brutally high temperature and was heavily jaundiced, to boot. There was no telling how much actual damage had been done to her liver. The good news, as Tom pointed out, was that we were talking about the one organ that could regenerate itself. It wasn't much to hold on to, but it was all we had.

By the next day, Dervish, the big orange-and-white guy, had come down with the same virus. The tests ruled out the three F's—feline leukemia, FIP, and FIV—which made it all the more puzzling. The other cats threw off the virus quickly, but Keisha stayed on at the clinic, attached to an I.V, for four and a half days, fighting for all she was worth. She came home the day after Labor Day. The jaundice was still there, but not as severe, and her

47

temperature had let up a little. It could still go either way, though. I had to feed her through a syringe seven to eight times a day and somehow get the Clavamox and her other meds down her as well.

"If anyone can pull her through this," Tom said, "you can."

The problem was, I didn't feel as confident of my abilities as he did. In the last year and half, we'd lost a number of cats, not just Keisha's little Siamese waifs, and all those deaths had, as someone phrased it, put my "heart in a pendulous place." An afraid-to-hope locked-in-limbo place, which is one of the closest things to hell on earth I've ever known.

I did everything I could think of, even clipping a little cat guardian-angel charm to Keisha's elegant purple collar. Couldn't hurt, I figured. Didn't seem to help much either, however. She was still very weak, still very far from turning that invisible corner. I couldn't bear the thought of this beautiful, vibrant cat dying. Finally, I sat down with her one night and, placing my hands on her, prayed with everything I was worth.

Then it happened.

An incredible current of energy shot through my fingertips and into Keisha's plush blue tortoiseshell fur. It was like nothing I had ever experienced before. Something—or, rather, Someone—was working through me. Like Emily Dickinson's afterlife, it was as "invisible, as music, but positive, as sound."

Shortly afterward, Keisha bit her feeding syringe in half. *Get that damned thing outta here,* she informed me, her pale-green eyes blazing. By the end of the month, her blood work came back normal. She'd fought the good fight and won.

Sometimes, when you're in a betwixt-and-between place, as Keisha undoubtedly was that night, when medicine has done all that it can, prayer and the sense that someone loves you very much and is pulling for you with every fiber of his or her being can tip the scales. I know I felt that current, and I believe that Keisha, sick as she was, felt it too.

By the way, she still wears the cat-angel charm on her collar, right over her name tag. Just a little reminder that faith—like ten-week-old kittens—shouldn't be discounted.

Old Friends

Dervish hops up next to me on the breezeway sofa. He purrs companionably while I have my morning coffee, then rests his large orange-and-white head on my wrist till it's time for me to get to work. He's fourteen pounds now—a far cry from his twenty-two-pound Great Pumpkin magnificence in his prime—and sometimes his thick coat gets matted and needs comb intervention. But those things don't matter between old friends.

We do go back a long time, Derv and I: It has been sixteen years since he came to us as a round-eyed rambunctious kitten that his first owner was eager to unload.

Later in the morning, I go upstairs to check on Zorro, who's sleeping in my daughter's room. The heat has been troubling him, and his appetite is a bit off. He peers up at me, purrs, and goes back to sleep. He, too, has lost weight and tone with age, and his sight is blurred from cataracts. We go back a long way, too, Zorro and I: it has been fifteen years since he wandered out of the woods by our old house, a fearless, friendly kitten-adventurer.

Derv and Zorro, along with Woody (a mere twelve-years -old and a former stray himself), are the last of the Old Guard. The rest of our feline familiars—a motley gang of Abyssinians, Siamese, and good ol' garden-variety mogs—are considerably younger. Oh, they're loving, exasperating personalities in their own right, with more idiosyncrasies than a whole slew of Dickens characters, and some day, they, too, will be the Old Guard. But Derv and Zorro were there almost from the beginning, even before my daughter, Marissa, was born.

Derv came to us when Tim and I had been married about two years. Actually, I snuck him into the house while Tim was taking part in a training program out in Milwaukee. At the time, we had just the two barn-cat sisters, Cricket and Kilah, and he was adamant about keeping it that way. So were the sisters, who'd gotten all bottle-brush-tailed about other cats we'd briefly taken care of for friends. In theory, I agreed with them.

I forgot all theory, however, when I saw the ad for a deaf kitten in need of a home. I could just picture him, all drooping whiskers and forlorn face like the sad-eyed kitten pictures of my childhood. Before I knew it, I was reaching for the phone.

The kitten who showed up in our kitchen that afternoon was white with a red-tabby mask and patches. He was so young that his eyes were still blue. He wasn't in the least pathetic— he began shadow-boxing with his reflection in the dishwasher door almost immediately—and there definitely wasn't anything wrong with his hearing.

What he was was absolutely adorable. Even Tim conceded as much when he came home from Milwaukee . . . right before he told me that the newcomer had to go. He even lined up a potential taker—his sister, Carolyn, who lived in New Hampshire.

Carolyn came down, took a look at the orange-and-white fur ball half-asleep in the laundry basket, asked him what he thought of the name "MacGyver"—and then suddenly concluded it was too hot that particular day to subject him to the long trip up north. By then, Dervish (Tim had given him the

51

name on account of his antics, especially his crimes against toilet paper) had been with us a few weeks; I think Carolyn, who misses very little, saw that he already had us in his over-sized paws. No more was ever said about a name change and transfer.

We still had a sizable problem to deal with, though. Derv, for all his calendar-kitten cuteness, was "wild for to hold" and clearly had tiger fantasies. Translated, he was a biter. *That,* and not his supposed deafness, we realized, was why his first owner had been so eager to send him on his way. One night, shortly after Carolyn's visit, Tim was lying on the sofa in his robe, telling me a story, when he suddenly yelped with pain. Within seconds, Derv scurried around the sofa and out into the kitchen, looking incredibly pleased with himself. He had snuck under Tim's robe and bit him on the butt: a real coup for a kitten.

Gradually, we were able to tame him. He remained ex-tremely playful, though, and the "Ladies of the Club"—Crick-et, Kilah, and Tikvah, an eighteen-month-old stray who'd re-cently joined their ranks—weren't. Then Zorro wandered into our yard and decided that any yard with a catnip bed that close to the birdfeeder (a poor miscalculation on my part) had real potential.

The wayfaring kitten was roughly eight weeks old and had suspiciously Abyssinian-looking ears, eyes, and coat to go with the charcoal-colored tabby stripes on his face, chest, and legs. I brought him into the kitchen and gave him some food and water; then, mindful that it hadn't been all that long since I'd gotten clearance for Tikvah, put him back outside. The kit-ten had ideas, though, and they did not include leaving. He kept returning to the back porch steps and working his expres-sive green eyes. You seem like such a nice human . . .

He worked his charms even harder when Tim came home

from work. My husband had just given him a temporary visa when the phone rang. Tim sat down on the loveseat to take the call, which happened to be work-related one, and Zorro, wide-eyed opportunist that he was, curled up confidingly on Tim's right shoulder and fell asleep. Tim was a cat person, and that melted him in nanoseconds. Zorro wasn't going anywhere.

Derv was delighted. He would lie in wait under a chair or the bed, stretch out a long white paw, and hook his new little buddy in. A glorious wrestling match would follow. Derv also displayed a curious paternal streak toward Zorro and would groom him before setting to work on his own fur. They'd spend hours together, napping companionably or stretched out by the windowsills on the enclosed back porch, no doubt discussing Zorro's adventures out in the wild, Tikvah's bossiness, or Derv's brief romance with Silver Bear, a beautiful stray who had gone to live with Carolyn, only to give birth to five kittens shortly afterward. (Carolyn always suspected Derv of having been the father—he'd met Silver Bear shortly before he was neutered—and threatened him with a paternity suit; I countered by saying that we'd have to haul Ms. Bear in for corrupting a minor).

They frequently joined forces. Once, a dear friend, Florence, came to lunch. Now Florence hadn't cared much for cats until two by the names of Blue and Jake had come into her life. Derv and Zorro were sitting on the kitchen table, clearly planning to join us. "You don't mind cats on the table, do you?" I asked sheepishly, as I hung her coat up on the cellar-door coat rack.

"I do mind cats on the table," Florence assured me. And that was that.

Or so I thought. We were eating lunch when I saw Florence's coat seemingly lift itself off the peg. Slowly, it began moving down the cellar steps like a thing possessed. And it was possessed, as I discovered when I rescued it: Derv, the larger of the two cats, was on the inside, doing the brunt of the work, and Zorro was helping his big buddy from the outside. God knows what they had planned for the coat.

Derv was the extrovert, the official greeter, and all-around huggable guy. He loved everybody, and everybody loved him. Once, I actually woke up to find him sleeping in between Tim and me, his grapefruit-sized head all nice and comfy on the pillow. As he grew into what my mother-in-law, Bobbie, called "a Portly Paws," he truly didn't mind if you used him as a pillow, provided that you rested just the side of your face ever so gently against his well-padded flank. Later, when Marissa appeared on the scene, Derv would lie in her Pack 'n Play with her, letting her put her tiny feet up on him.

Zorro, on the other hand, went from being a friendly, talky kitten—he used to make funny little *Nyeh-nyeh-nyeh* speeches to apprise us of his and Mr. Lion's whereabouts (Mr. Lion was a small toy animal that Zorro was fond of dragging about the house)—to being something of a brooding loner. Even though he wasn't a purebred, he developed a more than purebred attitude. Incredibly striking with his subtle mix of Abyssinian and tabby markings, he was "bad but beautiful," Bobbie declared (he'd clawed her stockings at their first meeting). He became very territorial, spraying anything that he felt needed reclaiming. Usually, that meant Tim's stuff, which obviously put a big strain on their relationship. Tim frequently rued the day that he'd fallen for the deceptively sweet-looking kitten asleep on his shoulder.

Yet for all his bad but beautiful ways, Zorro had a great gift: he was a paws-on healer. After I'd had a bad day, he would seemingly materialize out of nowhere and lie on my chest. The tension would ebb out of me almost immediately. At first, I wrote it off as my imagination; now that I've studied Reiki, I don't. Some people possess a healing touch—"golden hands," as my grandmother used to say—so why not Zorro? Cats are so alive to warmth, to the vibrations of worlds seen and unseen, that they're the perfect energy conductors.

Changes came to us. Woody and Boris, two other strays, joined us. We had Marissa. Then, when she was three and a half, Tim was killed in a car accident. All was, to paraphrase Yeats, changed, changed utterly. Six years later, we packed up our memories and animals and left the old house. By this time, several of our old-timers—Cricket, Tikvah, and Boris—had left us for celestial catnip beds (hopefully, from their perspective, with birdfeeders right next to them)—and others had come to ease the loneliness their going had left behind. And front and center were Kilah, Derv, and Zorro, who'd been with us from the beginning.

We lost Kilah to cancer two years after the move. But Derv and Zorro are still here, living, loving connections to that other time. They're thinner than they were, and they make a lot more trips to see our vet, Tom, than they used to. Derv needs to be dosed nightly for his megacolon condition. He is also considerably less patient with the younger cats, frequently retreating to his private lair (an old bureau/cabinet with one lower door missing and a fleecy orthopedic blanket inside) when their rowdiness gets on his nerves. Zorro spends part of each winter on Clavamox for his chronic upper-respiratory infections and no longer gets scolded for occasional spraying; his failing eyesight has given him a built-in alibi.

Derv, however, still fills the house with his presence. He inspects everything that's going on, purring loudly. He snores even more loudly; I can hear him snore several rooms away. Zorro, who has mellowed back into being the affectionate character who wandered out of the woods that summer day, continues to do his paws-on healing.

Sometimes I've put off writing about certain cats, and then suddenly they're gone, leaving only memory where once there were warm, purring presences. Anne in Margaret Campbell Barnes' *My Lady of Cleves* (a delightful but out-of-print novel, well worth looking up), reflects "that when people are parting it is best to speak straight from the heart lest one should withhold some ultimate tenderness until it be too late." Hopefully, it'll be a long while before Derv, Zorro, and I come to that seemingly final parting that's so hard to see beyond.

But old friends—endearing quirks, faulty lines, and all—still need to be celebrated. Sluggish colons, cataracts, chronic sinus problems (mine as well as Zorro's!), C-section scars, life lessons; we are all the worse—or the better—for wear, and that, as the Velveteen Rabbit learned, is when things become Real.

Heart & Soul

When Cricket died, I felt as if she'd taken her share of my heart with her. She'd been with me through marriage, motherhood, widowhood, and the launching of my career as a writer, and now, suddenly, she was gone. No loving cat presence hanging out at the computer with me or tripping the kitty fantastic down the stairs alongside me, waiting for me to sit down on the stairs with her and scritch the plush brownish-gray tiger fur she was so justifiably vain about. No understanding amber eyes or crackling purr to help me through the blue moods, the endless gray days. She had been my solace, my heart's ease, and, above all else, my Soul. And now that Soul had departed from my house, leaving it empty and echoing.

But there was still Tikvah—demanding, fearful, loyal, double-pawed Tikvah, who looked enough like Cricket to have been her littermate. She eased the pain following Cricket's death with her own funny, fierce devotion. I could never pick her up without her growing six extra paws and flailing about—a sign of the abuse she must've received in a previous life—but I could hold her in such a way that she came to understand that I wouldn't hurt her, and she followed me about like a four-footed shadow, carrying on a pretty constant stream of conversation. She taught me in her own way about love and its shadow side, fear—how sometimes you had to take hold of that fear to get to the love.

Three years later, Tikvah was gone, too. Oh, we had other cats—each one a quirky, colorful personality in his or her own right—but no one who was my special crony, as Cricket and Tikvah had been. Then Solstice stepped to the forefront.

Actually, she'd been doing her own little paw-shuffle

toward me even before Tikvah had died. Since Solstice had been a sickly kitten, I'd been feeding her by hand and fussing over her in general. It had built a bond between us, although I didn't realize how strong that bond was till she went up to my friend Mary's cattery in Rochester for an enforced honeymoon and ended up staying for three months. I missed her terribly; Solstice was homesick and not, she made it clear to her intended, that big on arranged marriages. She came home with her virginity intact and another, even bigger polyp in her throat.

She also came back knowing in her delicate little Abyssinian bones that she was my cat. When I opened the carrier that day, wondering if she'd even remember us, she bolted up out of the carrier into my lap, the love leaping out of her huge eyes—eyes that were as amber and glowing as my Cricket's had been.

Her next operation was a complete success; Tom was able to remove the entire polyp, and Solstice finally started gaining some desperately needed weight. Then she began to pick up where Cricket had left off, even adopting my old girl's habits of coming down the stairs with me a few steps at a time and helping with the weekly bed-changing—"helping" meaning, in her case, as it had in Cricket's, tunneling under the fresh sheets or leaping on them, ready for the kill, the moment I tried to straighten them out. Solstice had the same thoughtful understanding in her glance and her manner that Cricket did. It was as if my tigery old barn cat and this aristocratic little showgirl had somehow melded into one. I started calling her "Sol" for short, not even thinking about the pun or the truth therein.

Over time, though, it has come to me: she *is* my Soul, my kindred spirit in a fur suit, the one who will rush to my side when my world is askew and I have, in the words of the old song, "wounds to bind." She is my familiar in the best sense of the word, just as Cricket was.

Dawn came to us from Mary's cattery nine months after Solstice's last operation, just as winter was giving way to spring. I'd once joked that I wanted some day to adopt a black female cat and name her "D. B. Dawn"—"Darkest Before the Dawn"—but there was nothing dark about this Dawn. She was an incredibly petite Red Abyssinian female with just a touch of gold to her coat, and gold eyes that seemed almost too big for her pointy little face. She was skittish at first, as Solstice had been, but quickly came around, burrowing under the bedcovers and getting up close and personal with me when she felt like having a bit of company at night.

After her first heat, she returned to Mary's for breeding and stayed up there almost as long as Solstice had. Dawn came back pregnant and, just a couple of days before Valentine's Day, gave birth to a single Ruddy Aby kitten, Aspen, whose legs looked way too short for her furry butterball body. My daughter, Marissa, and I used to joke that pretty soon, Ms. Aspen would be so big, she'd be carrying her tiny mama around by the nape of *her* neck.

Aspen was an enchantment, no way around it. We willingly gave up hours every evening to kitten-watching, delighted when she opened her eyes and began to recognize us, cracking up when she and Dawn had endless squeak-and-squeal conversations in "the nursery" (the back spare room), or when she managed to squeeze her pudginess through the sizable gap under the door and escape into the hallway.

When Aspen died so suddenly, then, one March night—probably from a viral infection or a congenital defect, Tom said, although I chose not to have an autopsy done—she broke our hearts, and we mourned as though we'd lost a human baby. Dawn wandered through the house, making plaintive little cries that cut through us with stiletto sharpness. As heart-wrenching as those cries were, however, even worse were the times when she paced through the empty nursery not making a sound, her golden eyes puzzled and forlorn.

"She's trying to make sense of why all that happened," Maine-based animal healer Gigi Kast explained shortly afterward. "Even though the spiritual self was acquiescent, she has to deal with it on an emotional and physical level." Like us, she was learning a hard lesson in resiliency and in trusting the process.

Gradually, Dawn began to put on a little weight, to play with her toys again, and to run races with the other young cats. Her golden-red fur regained its gloss, and her eyes started to lose their brooding, searching look. Little more than a kitten herself, she was learning to be happy again, and she was all the more loving for what she had gone through.

Not long ago, Marissa came home from a tag sale with a little gray-and-white kitten-guy whom she promptly dubbed Gremlin. Dawn gave a perfunctory hiss, then sat back, her large gold eyes rapt. Spellbound. You could almost see her mulling it all over in her mind, weighing the possibilities that this anything-but-Abyssinian-looking kitten suggested. By evening, she had adopted him and was happily washing him. And Gremlin? He was trotting around adoringly after his new mom and squealing delightedly during their wrestling matches.

About a week later, Katherine, the little girl from whom we'd gotten Gremlin, came over to see how he was doing. I knew that her family was moving soon, and out of curiosity, I asked if they were taking the mother cat with them.

Katherine shook her head. "She ran away eight weeks ago. We can't find her."

So the kitten who had brought that glow back to Dawn's eyes had needed her as much as she had needed him. Each had filled the other's emptiness—each had given the other something to love.

If Solstice is my brand-new Soul, then Dawn is—not my Shadow or Shadow-self, as Tikvah was—but my Heart. We've both experienced motherhood, love, and loss and struggled our way through that last one. When she comes to me now and walks over my work, de- manding a head-scritch, or snuggles un- der the blankets next to me, purring, I can't help smiling to myself, no matter what kind of day it has been. She is not the Darkest-Before-the-Dawn cat that I once joked about, although she knows a lot about that particular brand of darkness. No, she is my Dawntreader, my Dawnstar, who has taught me about taking heart; about that heart being broken wide open, and about hope, faith, and joy taking root in it. Especially joy.

Storms Passing

*For Stormy (2000–2004), whose heart stopped
unexpectedly one June morning*

After a storm's passing,
the air is calm,
          almost considerate,
the colors sharper,
& the shore peaceful
          beyond reckoning.
But when you
          with your Ruddy Abyssinian
                    face, quizzical green eyes,
                    & playful, bounding spirit
          passed out of our lives
          so suddenly,
          so inexplicably,
          you left a grief
too big for us to hold.
Your afterglow
lingers, shimmering
          in the swishing field grasses
that you, an indoor cat,
could not explore;
in the yellowred&orange daylilies,
     almost as vibrant as you;
     in all places wild
          & untamable.
               You, with your cougar grace
          & satiny coat,
left us bereft
on a lonely shore,
     our world all the grayer
     for your going.

Woodruff X- Stray
For Tim

Woody lies next to me on the sofa, covering half of my writing portfolio with his black-spotted white body. *Going to write, were you?* his yellow eyes inquire. *I don't think so.* He has, he indicates gently, no plans of budging. *You may, however, pet me.*

That's Woody for you—low-key but persistent. He has a voice, all right, but he tends to save it for things that matter, such as sweet-talking susceptible humans into giving a young down-on-his-luck cat a home.

He was roughly eight months old when he wandered into my husband Tim's vegetable garden and good graces more than thirteen years ago—definitely feral but friendly, too, and more than willing to pass the time with a sociable human. He started visiting Tim on a regular basis. I was aware of him; we had a slew of strays coming into our yard that year, but Woody stood out by virtue of those huge spots on his dazzling white fur. He acknowledged me—I was, after all, the bringer of food—but he zeroed in on Tim. Smart move, seeing as my husband was the one he'd have to get clearance from.

We had five cats then, and Tim was pretty adamant about there being no more room at the inn. So I kept quiet, put out food for the strays, and worried about them when the weather was bad.

"You know, that is a nice cat," Tim observed one day after a visit from his black-and-white buddy. "Really friendly."

"Oh."

Maybe a week later, Tim said casually, "Wonder if he

belongs to anyone." He paused. "Maybe we should kidnap him."

Within days of that conversation, Woody was in the house. An outdoorsy name seemed called for, so I named him "Woodruff" after the white-flowered herb in my garden; Tim, who loved punning, added the "X. Stray."

Woodruff X. Stray liked me. He liked our eight-month-old daughter, Marissa, though there was probably a slightly ulterior motive mixed in with his liking, especially as she moved on to solid foods. When she graduated to chopped-up hot dogs, the former stray positioned himself faithfully by her high chair and waited for fallout: *This is great. Wait till the old gang outside hears about this.* Then, after days and days of hot-dog fallout, Woody finally walked away. *I will eat no more hot dogs forever,* the dismissive swish of his plumy black tail said.

Not that the hotdog incident interfered with his liking of Marissa. He was, as I've said, a very sociable guy and liked to greet everybody. Once, my mother-in-law was babysitting Marissa. While Marissa was napping, Bobbie—who believed, she always said, in "letting sleeping babies lie"—made herself comfortable in the gooseneck rocker with a magazine. Suddenly, out of nowhere, came Woody. He jumped up on her lap, and then, realizing they hadn't been Properly Introduced, licked her right on the lips and high-tailed it down. *Mustn't overdo this interspecies thing.*

However, Woody was, first and foremost, Tim's cat. Tim had taken him in. Tim was the one he followed about. Of course, Tim was also the one he stole food from on a regular basis. A good-natured con, Woody was never one to let affection interfere with business. One evening, Tim dallied out in the yard, talking to neighbors instead of coming right in for dinner. I grew tired of waiting—when Tim was telling a story, God couldn't have shut him up—so I left his chicken pie on the table and went upstairs to put Marissa to bed. "How was the pie?" I asked absently over my book when he came up much later.

"The *crust*"—Tim mustered up all the sarcasm he could, which was considerable—"was fine."

"The crust?" I looked up blankly.

"I thought you'd taken the filling out because I was late for dinner," he explained sheepishly.

I shook my head. "I might've yelled at you," I said, "but I wouldn't have *starved* you."

The real culprit was soon discovered, and not too far away from the crime scene. Woody had Hoovered out every last smidgen of chicken-pie filling, leaving just the crust. Crust was fattening, he assured us, as he finished meticulously cleaning his paws.

He took to sitting on the table, right next to Tim's plate. In fact, he was such a regular, Tim began to comment on his absences. "Woody's not here," my husband would say, staring suspiciously at his meal. "I'm not eating."

Woody's thievery and klutziness aside—whenever the "cow cat" jumped up on the bookcase or a bureau, he inevitably took down a few ornaments and pictures with that long plumy tail of his—Tim loved him. "Just looking at him," he'd say, "makes me smile."

Then Tim was killed in a car accident, and Woody, the loving and lovable, withdrew into himself. I was so overwhelmed by the tragedy and by having to suddenly raise Marissa by myself, I didn't notice it right away. When I did, I saw eyes as full of sadness as any human's, and I tried to make up for all the time he'd been left to grieve by himself.

Gradually, he transferred his affection to me. Then Star came into his life—an uppity ten-week-old Sealpoint Siamese that an old friend had given me. Star, who was missing mom and the littermates, took one look at Woody and latched right on to him. And I do mean "latched"; I'd wake up to weird noises in the night and find her at the foot of my bed, nursing on him. I'm still not sure why Woody let her do it. Perhaps it had to do with the fact that he was still feeling very vulnerable. Maybe Star just didn't listen to his objections and went ahead and did what she wanted. She's like that.

Whatever the reason, they soon became an item. And an item they have remained to this day, Star snuggling up against Woody one moment and cuffing him without warning the next. It's a challenging relationship, further complicated by the fact that Woody now has the biggest crush on our littlest cat, Dawn. He is caught between a Siamese and an Abyssinian, and, as he tells us in plaintive miaows, that is infinitely harder than being caught between an old rock and a hard place—especially when the Siamese is Star. On the whole, though, he is happy, as he tells me now in a series of burbling purrs. There's a goodly sprinkling of white hairs on his black ears—courtesy of Star, we assume—but I don't mention those.

The phone rings, so I have to get up, upsetting both Woody and the notebook. I come back a little later and get back on the sofa, ready to return to my rough draft. Before I can pull the notebook over to me, however, Woody is on it. Literally. He is now covering the whole portfolio, not just half of it. He glances up at me, his yellow eyes shining. Tim was right: just looking at him makes me smile.

Soul-Cat

She talks to me with her eyes—those incredibly sweet almond-shaped amber eyes. It's an Aby trick: even Zorro, our half-Abyssinian cat, does it. Solstice, my Ruddy girl, has never used her voice much until now.

She scarfs down some chicken, then wanders down to the cellar. A little later, when my daughter, Marissa, and I are sitting at the picnic table in the backyard, I glance up to see Solstice sitting in the kitchen window. *Just wanted to know where you were*, her eyes say as they shift from honey amber to moss amber and back again to honey.

My beloved Soul-Cat is dying. She is only five -years -old, but she's in kidney failure, the bane of so many Abyssinians. I don't know exactly how much longer we have together, only that every moment is achingly precious.

Until a few weeks ago, we had no idea that she was in danger. We were treating her for a badly abscessed tooth, and she seemed to be responding to the antibiotics. One day, I found a cat fang lying on Marissa's bureau and figured that that was the end of Solstice's problem tooth.

Then I noticed that she'd lost her cougar sleekness. Her beautiful Ruddy coat with its apricot underbelly suddenly felt as loose and woolly as the jacket an old beau had given me. Nice in the jacket, but somehow not quite right in the Aby.

That's when a trip to the emergency vet clinic revealed the underlying problem. Both my heart and mind fought the news. Solstice had been my little miracle cat: I had hand-fed her as a sickly kitten and seen her through two surgeries for throat polyps when she'd been just a year old. She, in turn, had made

67

it clear—by following me up and down the stairs and performing kitty Reiki or push-paws on me when I was resting—that she was a one-person cat, and I was that one person.

This time, I know, there will be no miracle for my Solstice. But we do not have to say good-bye just yet.

The other cats seem to understand that Solstice is ill, but take the matter in their furry stride. They sit with her on the kitchen counter, watching the birds at the feeders together, or sun themselves with her in the breezeway.

Marissa and I have gotten the hydrating-and-medicating process down pretty well now. I'm feeding Solstice baby food—sometimes from a spoon, sometimes from my fingers—and Nutri-Cal. Her coat has regained some of its gloss, although it still has a rumpled dandruff-y look. Tom sees an improvement in her attitude, if not in her kidney values; at her last visit, she kicked over our over-stuffed file folder and looked smug as the tech was picking up the papers, as if to say, *See what happens when you mess with me? Don't you ever think about sticking me with that thermometer again.* "She is," Tom says, "a scrappy cat despite her condition . . . I wouldn't give up hope."

Still, there's a certain amount of letting go I have to do. Little rituals—our going up and down stairs together a few steps at a time, or my giving her the corn silk and shucks to play with when we're having fresh corn—have to be put aside now that her energy level is so much lower. No more Solstice playing cave kitty in the sheets while I'm changing the bed. No more doing her kitty Reiki. No more glancing down when I wake up in the middle of the night to see her sleeping in the cubbyhole of my night table.

Now I do Reiki on her, scritching her ears when she's up for it and letting her rest when she's not. On her good days, Solstice sits there, her almond-shaped eyes glowing. I assure her that she is still beautiful — that she still has my heart.

Her eyes deepen. *Of course,* they say. *You gave it to me a long time ago. No take-backs.*

No take-backs. For all the pain of letting her go, I wouldn't have it any other way. Love is, as the "Song of Songs" says, strong as death. Stronger. And therein lies the miracle.

One night, just before I head upstairs, I go over to Solstice, who's resting on the kitchen counter. Gently, I pat her. She turns toward me and begins rubbing her face against my hand. She keeps doing this till there's almost a kind of rhythm to it. *Love you, too,* the big amber eyes say. *My human.* When I move over to the other side of the counter, she makes herself get up and follow me. Then she begins nuzzling my hand all over again. It's as if she can't stop. Won't stop.

The next day, she's so congested, she can't even smell her baby food. Depressed, I go out to run errands, anything to escape the pain threatening to overtake me. Ten minutes down the road, I hear a voice say, "Go back." And, like Solstice the night before, it doesn't let up.

Finally, I turn around and go home. I give Solstice her antibiotic early, figuring that it might just break up the congestion enough for her to eat. It works. She manages to get some shredded chicken down, then rubs her head against my hand. *Thank you. You came back for me. You always do.*

My heart still does a horrible lurch inside me when I look at her and see a little ghost-cat where not so very long ago, there was a beautiful Ruddy cougar of an Aby. But I'm suddenly glad that I listened to that voice—that I went back and faced the pain instead of running from it.

When I bring her in to see my vet, Tom, the next morning, her mouth has become necrotic. She's anemic, and there's a strong uremic odor permeating her coat. Once a sleek nine and a half pounds, she now weighs about as much as a six-month-old kitten.

Tom can't find a vein on her, so he gives her a slow-working abdominal injection. Then we wrap Solstice gently in a towel. "I'm so sorry," I tell her, my eyes and voice clogged with tears.

"You did everything you could," Tom says. He sighs. "I really thought she had a chance. She put up a good fight." He leaves the room so I can have the remaining time—maybe ten minutes or so—alone with her, to hold and talk to her.

Solstice squirms at first. Affectionate as she is, she doesn't care much for being held. Finally, she settles down in my arms. I talk to her, even pray a little.

Slowly, Solstice puts her head down on my breast and keeps it there. I never know the exact instant that she dies, only that the room is suddenly awash with peace and love. By holding her till the end and then some—by going with her as far on her journey as I can—death has somehow changed its shape and is no longer a cruel, fearsome bogey to shrink from. This is just one more gift that she has given me.

*****

But not the last. About a week later, I'm out in my backyard, raking. Suddenly, I see Solstice. Every detail is as finely limned as in a painting. She's sitting at the edge of my meditation garden, beautiful and glowing in her autumnal colors. I can even see the silky apricot underbelly that she loved having stroked. Her tail is wrapped around her paws, and she simply radiates love and happiness. I can almost hear her burble.

The image keeps coming in, stronger and stronger. For the first time since I learned that she was dying, I feel happy. Or, rather, I can feel her happiness as though it was my own. It's as though she's inside me, and not just figuratively: a physical warmth suffuses me.

She keeps appearing to me in the weeks that follow. I'll be

70

out driving, or raking, or walking, and suddenly, she's there. In ghostly tales, you know a spirit is present because of the eerie chill that cuts through you. But with Solstice, there is only that incredible inrush of warmth.

A long time ago, I christened Solstice my "House Blessing" because her complete recovery from her throat polyps marked the end of a sad, dark time when we'd lost several beloved family pets. And, truly, ever since our souls touched and melded more than five years ago, everything about Solstice has been a blessing or a miracle to me. Even now, it seems, my little cat has a miracle or two up her paw.

All at once, I get it. The miraculous is always around us: it's just that the nature of the miracles changes. Many of them are as quiet and understated as a loving amber-eyed Abyssinian who used to wait for me to come in from my morning run. We only know they're miracles because of that feeling of "unexpected grace" that they inevitably bring with them—the way they stop time and reveal the soul of things.

My House Blessing is still with me, as magical as roses in November, and as real. The body is gone, but the spirit is more than willing.

Leaps of Faith

He is not show quality. His hind feet are oversized, clearly designed for a larger cat. He is a toilet-paper shredder, and wallpaper-border and wire chewer. (He took down a mini-stereo, and the electrified houses in our miniature Halloween village gave up their low-wattage ghosts and spooky lights shortly after his arrival). Knickknacks that the other cats ignore—my mother-in-law's little hand-painted wooden eggs from India, for instance—are, to his Aby way of thinking, toys for the taking. (The eggs make great noises when he knocks them apart and chases the halves along the floor). He is not graceful, and has more failed counter jumps than not to his credit. As for bathtubs . . . "When hasn't he fallen in?" my fourteen-year-old daughter, Marissa, observes sarcastically.

All of this has in no way stopped Phoenix from trying. He is a great believer in leaps of faith. OK, so he frequently slam-dunks himself into the kitchen floor. But sometimes—especially when it counts, like at feeding time—he does conquer the counter. Clearly, he doesn't care to dwell on the misses. Onward and upward is his motto—even if he does end up downward and splay-pawed a few times first.

Phoenix came to us following my beloved Solstice's death. Shortly after our vet, Tom, confirmed that Solstice's kidneys were failing rapidly, I contacted Mary at Aby Central—known to the outside world as Singin' Cattery—in Rochester, New York. Once Solstice was gone, we would be without a Ruddy Abyssinian, and I couldn't bear the thought. I love the Aby in all its colors, but something about the Ruddys with their cougar grace and warm autumnal coloring had always especially appealed to me. Did Mary have any pet-quality Ruddys?

Mary did. A year-old already neutered male who, she said, needed more love than she could give him, given the demands of the cattery. She would keep him for us until our vigil with Solstice was over.

The end of that vigil came much sooner than we had expected. About a month later, we found ourselves driving home with one highly indignant Aby male. He wasn't loud like a Siamese, of course—I don't think that the Abys can hit those piercing Yoko Ono notes that their Siamese brethren can—but he was pretty insistent, nonetheless. Since I was concentrating on the highway, I missed the gist of his plaintive commentary, but I'm pretty sure he said something about contacting Interpol.

Still, Phoenix seemed to settle in reasonably well once we got home. Abys are fairly group-oriented, and Celtie and Rory accepted him matter-of-factly. Dawn was a little less charitable. Following Solstice's death, the tiny Red Aby had become my No. 1 familiar—I think that Solstice had left me to Dawn in her Will—and she said awful things to the newcomer in that soft chittering voice of hers.

Not that Phoenix noticed. He was delightfully oblivious to her natterings and hisses and happily bopped along with the Younger Gang—Gremlin, Rory, and Hawkeye. In fact, he soon decided that Hawkeye, who was about the same age, was his long-lost littermate. The fact that Hawkeye, with his silver-streaked black fur, wouldn't have passed for an Aby in any universe didn't trouble Phoenix in the least. They had, Phoenix informed his new bro, been separated at birth, probably by (this was said with a quick glance at Star, whom Phoenix had enough sense to be wary of) an Evil Siamese.

No foolin,' said Hawkeye, who was very impressed by this upgrade in his pedigree.

It's true, Phoenix assured him, and proceeded to paw-wrestle him to the floor. After all, what else were brothers for?

On the whole, it felt as though we were in for a relatively peaceful transition. I was shocked, then, when Phoenix developed a food allergy and kicked and scratched so much, he began looking more like a moth-eaten teddy bear than a miniature cougar. I changed the cats' diet, working in some lamb baby food because, according to Tom, that was about as hypoallergenic as you could get. I dabbed Phoenix with every salve and ointment imaginable; when those didn't work, I took him in to the veterinary clinic for steroid shots.

It felt like a never-ending battle, particularly coming as it did right after Solstice's last illness. I found myself missing her more than ever. Solstice, for all her shyness, had been deeply loving, shadowing me up and down the stairs and sharing all sorts of silly, playful rituals with me. You know—the kind you have when you've been together a long time and know each other inside-out. Phoenix was friendly enough but came across as being more of a cat's cat and not all that interested in people.

That shows how wrong I was on all counts. The little Ruddy guy with the big feet was actually having more trouble getting adjusted to his new environment than I realized, And he was trying, in the only way he could, to tell me. What I couldn't see was that I was so locked in grief, I was unconsciously expecting him to be Solstice.

Gradually, as I rubbed salve into his raw hairless spots and spoon-fed him baby food, we began to bond. He took to hanging out on the stairs with me and burbling away, just as Solstice had. He began sleeping on my bed and doing push-paws or kitty Reiki on me, just as she had, albeit a lot more boisterously. He had a kitten-ish quality that Solstice never had—probably because she had been so ill her first year—and became so affectionate, I couldn't believe I'd ever called him "a cat's cat."

One day around the end of his second month with us, we laughingly watched him spring up and try to catch the raindrops hitting the long glass panel of the breezeway door. I knew then that Phoenix was more than just a replacement Ruddy—he was just as magical as his name.

What made him so magical was his ability to love, no holds barred. Once he felt more secure with us, he loved being picked up and held like a baby. He'd simply stand upright on his back legs and place his front paws on me: *Hugs now.* It became quite a ritual with him, particularly in the mornings. Didn't matter if he'd just gotten yelled at for crimes against toilet paper and wallpaper border. Didn't matter if I'd just let loose a banshee shriek because he'd taken a flying leap for me and dug those grappling hooks of his in my side. He'd just stare up at me with those greenish-gold eyes (Solstice's had been deep amber) and rear up on his hind feet, ready for lift-off: *Whatever. Hugs now, please.*

You see, Phoenix now had faith—faith that there would always be a pair of loving arms ready to catch him. And if the human attached to those arms sometimes shrieked or scolded… well, Humans Were Like That Sometimes, and You Couldn't Take Them Too Seriously.

No, he wasn't much like Solstice, who had had a tendency to hold back. Yet . . . one day, Phoenix was sniffing around some takeout I'd just picked up. I thought he was after Marissa's chicken parmagian, which he was very fond of, but then I realized that he wanted the crust off Marissa's peanut-butter-and-chocolate pie. So I broke off a few crumbs, making sure that there was no chocolate stuck to them, and he scarfed them up. I gave him a few more—same thing. Then I remembered.

Solstice had loved peanut butter from the time she was a sickly kitten. Somehow, even with the polyps she had in her

75

throat back then, she could swallow it easily, so I used to give her an occasional teaspoon—one of our many little rituals. Now, as Phoenix practically inhaled those peanut butter crumbs, my grief finally slipped quietly out the breezeway door. Phoenix was the perfect successor to Solstice, after all. I could just see the movie title on an imaginary marquee: "Son of Solstice." All I had ever really needed to do *was* make my own leap of faith toward him.

Phoenix has been with us a year and a half and is free of food allergies now. He is as loving and clueless and spazzy-pawed as ever, and I am still throwing out mutilated toilet-paper rolls. He is still performing acupuncture without a license. But on the plus side, I get hugs from a loving, impetuous Aby every morning, and I've learned a lot about leaping.

About the Author

T. J. Banks is the author of *Souleiado and Houdini,* a novel for young adults which the late writer and activist Cleveland Amory enthusiastically branded "a winner." Her work has appeared in numerous journals and anthologies, including *Soul Menders, Their Mysterious Ways, The Simple Touch of Fate, A Cup of Comfort for Women in Love, Chicken Soup for the Single Parent's Soul,* and Guideposts' *Comfort from Beyond series.* A Contributing Editor to *laJoie* and former stringer for the Associated Press, she has received awards for her work from the *Cat Writers' Association* (CWA), *ByLine,* and *The Writing Self.* She lives with her daughter, Marissa, and their cats and rabbits in a sometimes peaceable but always interesting kingdom in Connecticut.